Cleveland Radio Players

Sweetwater Files: Private instigator

Original Adaption and Performances

Originally adapted for the radio and performed by
The Cleveland Radio Players. Directed by Jim
Pelhyes. Recorded at Bad Racket Studios.

Starring:

Denny Castiglione	The Voice of The Cleveland Radio Players
Jack Matuszewski	Sylvester Sweetwater
Milton Horowitz	Giovanni Manetti
Dina Karalnik	Miss Rivers
Sonia Restivo	Miss Jamison
Eric Sever	Malcolm Ainsworth
Giovanni Castiglione	Carlie
David Flynt	Darren
Barnabas Brennan	Pete

OPENING CREDITS

          THE VOICE OF THE CLEVELAND RADIO PLAYERS
Hello... This is The Voice of The
Cleveland Radio Players... my name is
Denny Castiglione ladies and
gentlemen...

                              OPENING FANFARE

and you're listening to the Cleveland
Radio Players performance of The
Sweetwater Files written and directed
by Jimmy Pelyhes, Starring!...

          JACK MATUSZEWSKI
          DINA KARALNIK
          MILTON HOROWITZ
          ERIC SEVER
          SONIA RESTIVO
          GIOVANNI CASTIGLIONE
          BARNABAS BRENNAN
          DAVID FLYNT

This episode of Sweetwater Files:
Private Investigator, starts right
now...

                              FADE OUT

SWEETWATER AND KELP LAW OFFICES

                              TYPING SFX

                              PAPARAZZI SFX

                              DOOR OPENS

                              SOMEONE ENTERS

          RIVERS
How can I help--- (shocked,
stammering)

Oh my! You're...you're Heather
Jamison, the movie star. How...? What
are you---?

                    JAMISON
I'm filming a movie here in town.

                    RIVERS
Wow. I had no idea you were here.

                    JAMISON
Then you're the only one. The media
will not leave me alone.

                    RIVERS
How can I help you?

                    JAMISON
I need to see Mr. Sweetwater. Is he
in?

                    RIVERS
Yes. He's with his associate, Mr.
Manetti, but I'm sure he won't mind
the interruption.

                                    INTERCOM BUZZER

                    RIVERS
            (into intercom)
Mr. Sweetwater, Miss Heather Jamison,
the movie star, is here to see you.

                    SWEETWATER
            (from intercom)
Really, Heather Jamison, the movie
star... to see me?... Have her take a
seat. I'm meeting with George Clooney
right now, and Meryl Streep is coming
in at ten.

                    RIVERS
            (into intercom)
No, really. Come out and see for
yourself.

                    SWEETWATER
            (from intercom)
If it is her, I don't want to see her.
I'll send Manetti.

                                    FOOTSTEPS

                                    DOOR OPENS

                    MANETTI
              (calling to Sweetwater)
Hey boss, its-a Head-er Jamison all
right.

                    SWEETWATER
              (from inside his office)
Are you sure?

                    MANETTI
              (calling to Sweetwater)
Hang on. (to Jamison)

Are you Head-er Jamison?

                    JAMISON
Yes I am.

                    MANETTI
              (calling to Sweetwater)
Its-a her all right.

                    SWEETWATER
              (from inside his office)
Well I'm not speaking to her. She
never answered any of my letters.

                    JAMISON
Oh dear, I really need his help.

                    MANETTI
              (calling to Sweetwater)
She joosta said dose letters is da
reason she's-a here.

                    JAMISON
              (whispering to Manetti)
I never said that.

                    MANETTI
You no wanna him to come out?

                                    DOOR OPENS

                          FOOTSTEPS-RUNNING

                    SWEETWATER
Heather, darling! You're here to
accept my proposal. Now after we're
married, you keep making money...er, I
mean movies, and I'll be a stay-at-

home husband.

                    MANETTI
          Hey, Miss Jamison, you should-a no
          marry-a Sweetwater, he's-a no gonna
          stay at home.

                    JAMISON
          Gentlemen, I need help.

                    SWEETWATER
          Oh now I see, you're one of those
          "It's all about me" types... Well
          there is no "I" in marriage.

                    JAMISON
          Actually there is.

                    SWEETWATER
          Not even married yet and you're
          already correcting me. The wedding is
          off.

                    JAMISON
          Please---

                    SWEETWATER
          Begging won't help.

                    JAMISON
          If you would just---

                    SWEETWATER
          The best thing you can do now is just
          turn and walk away.

                    JAMISON
          Will you please shut up so I can
          finish a sentence?

                    SWEETWATER
               (indignant)
          Well, I never!

                    MANETTI
          Atsa right, he never shuts-a up.

                    JAMISON
          Maybe it was a mistake coming here.

                    MANETTI
Atsa what his clients say. But usually
after da trial.

                    RIVERS
How can we help you, Miss Jamison?

                    JAMISON
I need some legal advice.

                    MANETTI
Whattya need to know?

                    SWEETWATER
Ah Manetti, if you don't mind. I'll
handle this. She asked for legal
advice. If she needs advice on how to
hotwire a car, then we'll ask you.

                    JAMISON
Can I sue someone for having a big
mouth?

                    SWEETWATER
If you're referring to Manetti, you
gotta stand in line.

                    JAMISON
Actually it's someone in my entourage.

                    MANETTI
You wanna sue somebody in-a you car?

                    RIVERS
An entourage isn't a car, Mr. Manetti.
It's a group of people that work for
her.

                    JAMISON
And I think there's a leak---

                    MANETTI
Oh, you car gotta flat tire?

                    JAMISON
No, not that kind of leak---

                    MANETTI
Leek, like-a da onion? You can keep
it. I no like-a dem.

                    JAMISON
No. I mean---

                    SWEETWATER
Maybe it's a leak under her kitchen
sink.

                    JAMISON
          (increasingly frustrated)
Why can't I finish a sent---

                    MANETTI
I no tink a kitchen can-a sink.

                    SWEETWATER
My uncle had a sunken living room.

                    MANETTI
Really?

                    SWEETWATER
And a sunken living room, sunken den,
sunken bathroom... the big flood back
in '78.

                    JAMISON
          (angrily)
I think someone has been leaking info
about me to the media for quite
awhile. I haven't had a good role for
years.

                    MANETTI
Dats-a too bad. I run down to da
bakery on da corner, and-a get you a
sweet-a roll.

                    RIVERS
She didn't mean a roll you eat. She
meant a role in a movie.

                    MANETTI
You can eat rolls in da movie. You
just gotta sneak-a dem past da usher!

Jamison sighs loudly

                    JAMISON
The rumors have gotten more frequent
since I got the role in this movie.
There has been something in the media
every day. It's maddening.

                    SWEETWATER
Don't you think you're over-reacting?

                    JAMISON
     (angry)
I am not over acting! Why does
everyone say I'm over acting?

                    SWEETWATER
Have you seen any of your films?

                    JAMISON
My career will be ruined.

                    SWEETWATER
Maybe it's all in your head.

                    JAMISON
It's not in my head. Someone leaked
that I was coming here. There's a guy
that followed me, outside right now.

                    SWEETWATER
Let me handle... wait, is he a big
guy?... Manetti---

                    JAMISON
No, he's not big at all. He's smaller
than you.

                    SWEETWATER
Hold on Manetti. I'll take care of
this. And if I find him... You said "a
small guy" right?... I'll get rid of
him.

                    RIVERS
What if he has a gun or something?

                    MANETTI
Da boss-a he no scared-a guns, are ya
boss?

SWEETWATER
Of course I'm not scared of guns...
However, I am a little worried about
bullets.

JAMISON
He doesn't have a gun. He's Roger
McNamara from that TV gossip show,
"Celebrity Watch".

SWEETWATER
Then I'll need a gun.

FOOTSTEPS WALKING AWAY

DOOR OPENING AND CLOSING

RIVERS
Before you can even think about suing,
you have to find out who's the source.
You'll need a private detective.

MANETTI
I'm-a private detective. I gotta da
office and everyting.

JAMISON
You're a licensed private detective?

MANETTI
Sure here's-a my card.

JAMISON
        (reading the card)
"Giovanni Manetti... Licensed Private
Detective, No really, I am."

MANETTI
Atsa pretty impressive-a card, eh?

JAMISON
Well, licensed has a "c" in it; and
private ends in "e". Other than that---

MANETTI
Hey, you want-a someone dat can-a
spell or someone dat can-a snoop?

                    JAMISON
          I suppose I do need a detective. What
          are your rates?

                    MANETTI
          I gotta da rate to remain silent. I
          gotta the rate to an attorn---

                    JAMISON
          No, how much do you charge?

                    MANETTI
          I can no charge. Dey took-a my credit
          card.

Jamison lets out a exasperated sigh.

                    JAMISON
          Let me think about it.

                    RIVERS
          Do you really suspect someone in your
          entourage?

                    JAMISON
          It has to be one of them. Maybe one of
          my new communication assistants.

                    RIVERS
          Communication assistants?

                    JAMISON
          The people who handle my fan mail, so
          I don't have to deal with the crazies.
          Like last year, they said that some
          guy sent me a photo of himself in his---
           um,---birthday suit.

                    MANETTI
          How dey know it-a was his-a birtday?

The girls giggle.

                    RIVERS
          Mr. Manetti, a birthday suit means
          you're not wearing any clothes.

                    MANETTI
          He went-a to his birtday party naked?

                    JAMISON
          Anyway, I hope Mr. Sweetwater doesn't
          have any trouble with that McNamara
          guy. He is short, but I heard he was a
          navy seal.

                    MANETTI
          Den Sweetwater shoulda brought some
          fish. Seals like-a dem.

Girls giggle again.

                    RIVERS
          Mr. Manetti, a navy seal is someone
          trained for special dangerous
          missions.

                    JAMISON
          They're experts in hand to hand
          combat... Maybe I should have told
          that to Mr. Sweetwater.

                    MANETTI
          No, den he would-a sent me.

                                        DOOR OPENS

                                        SWEETWATER ENTERS

                    JAMISON
          Was he out there?

                    SWEETWATER
          I think so. I never got outside.

                    RIVERS
          What happened?

                    SWEETWATER
          It's raining. And these suede shoes
          are brand new... But I'll tell you
          this, it's too bad it's raining...

                    MANETTI
          Why, he gotta suede shoes too?

                    JAMISON
          I don't want him following me back to
          my hotel. That's the one secret I've
          been able to keep.

                    SWEETWATER
          Okay, here's what we'll do. Manetti,
          change coats with her. Then I'll take
          her out the back way to my car.

                    RIVERS
          So if that guy sees her, he'll think
          it's Mr. Manetti.

                    SWEETWATER
          Exactly.

                    MANETTI
          Atsa no good boss.

                    RIVERS
          Why?

                    MANETTI
          Her coat is-a no gonna fit me.

                                        TRANSITIONAL MUSIC

SWEETWATER AND KELP LAW OFFICES

                                        PHONE RINGS

Rivers answers.

                    RIVERS
          Sweetwater and Kelp Attorneys at Law.

                                        PAPER RATTLING

                    RIVERS
          We now have dozens of client comments
          online. Go to w-w-w dot- County Jail
          dot com keyword Sweetwater... What?

No, this is a law office... No, we're
not, we're a law office... What do you
mean, "Am I sure"?--- Fine, go ahead
order a pizza. You're not going to get
it.

                              PHONE HANG UP

                              INTERCOM BUZZES

          RIVERS
          (into intercom)
Mr. Manetti, you're using your
intercom.

          MANETTI
          (from intercom)
Is-a dat what dis is? No wonder it-a
no sharpen my pencil.

                              DOOR OPENS

Manetti walks out.

          RIVERS
There's something bothering me about
this Jamison case---

          MANETTI
Me-a too.

          RIVERS
I'm bothered by the fact that until
these last few weeks there was nothing
about her in the media for years. Is
that what's bothering you too?

          MANETTI
I was-a gonna say that-a I can no wear-
a her coat, its-a too itchy. But I
guess dat its-a all part of bein' a
detective.

          RIVERS
I was pleasantly surprised to hear
that you're a licensed detective. I
didn't even know you were taking the
classes.

          MANETTI
Ah, whadda you mean-a classes? I no

take-a classes. Dats a racket.

                    RIVERS
Mr. Manetti, you can't call yourself
licensed if you don't have a license.

                    MANETTI
I gotta da license... I go see my
friend Paulie at da pool hall. He sell-
a me one for-a ten dollars.

                                    DOOR OPENS

                                    FOOTSTEPS

                    RIVERS
Mr. Sweetwater, how did things go at
the hotel?

                    SWEETWATER
Fine... But if someone from the hotel
should happen to call, tell them that
statue was broken before I leaned into
it.

                    RIVERS
You broke one of those statues at the
Crown Legacy Hotel? They're priceless!

                    MANETTI
Good ting dey gotta no price.

                    SWEETWATER
Oldest trick in the book. Put a bunch
of crumbly old statues around and wait
for someone like me to show up. And we
all know what happens next.

                    MANETTI
Yeah, you knock-a dem over.

                    SWEETWATER
They fall over, and they sue me.

                    MANETTI
You gonna need da good lawyer. You
know any?

                    SWEETWATER
There were photographers and TV people
all over us when we got there. Lights

and cameras everywhere.

                    RIVERS
          That's horrible!

                    SWEETWATER
          People pushing and shoving. Reminded
          me of dinner at Manetti's.

                    RIVERS
          I guess there really is a leak.

                    SWEETWATER
          It appears so. Now how do we find out
          who it is?

                    MANETTI
          We need da private instigator like-a
          me.

Miss Rivers giggles.

                    RIVERS
          It's not instigator...it's---

Sweetwater interrupts her.

                    SWEETWATER
          Now, now Miss Rivers! Let's not be
          hasty! When Manetti's right, he's
          right!

                    RIVERS
          Poor, poor, Miss Jamison. I feel so
          bad for her.

                    SWEETWATER
          I think I'm falling for her.

                    MANETTI
          Now I feel-a bad for-a her.

                    SWEETWATER
And she's falling for me. I can see it
in her eyes---behind those sunglasses.
My single days will soon be over.

                    MANETTI
Before you start-a payin her alimony,
maybe you should-a go steady, or on-a
date or someting.

                    SWEETWATER
Good idea, Manetti.

                    MANETTI
You gonna call-a her?

                    SWEETWATER
No need. We're meeting her on the
movie set tomorrow morning at 7 AM.

                    MANETTI
I no wake-a up til 8.

                    SWEETWATER
Good. That means you'll be quiet for
at least an hour.

                                TRANSITIONAL MUSIC

CITY STREET LOCATION FOR FILMING

                                STREET SOUNDS

MALCOLM AINSWORTH the director is looking for Heather.

                    AINSWORTH
          (British accent)
Where is Heather Jamison?

                    WOMAN 1
          (from a distance)
She's still in make-up.

                    AINSWORTH
That's ruddy great! We're already
behind schedule. I mean, I'm only the
director. Okay, let's set up for the

next scene. Where's Scott Tyler?

                    WOMAN 1
The actor?

                    AINSWORTH
No, Scott Tyler, my bloody dry
cleaner! Of course the actor!

                    WOMAN 1
He's in his trailer.

                    AINSWORTH
Go get him.

                    WOMAN 1
He won't come to out until after
Heather Jamison shows up first. He
says that he's never the first one on
set. He's temperamental.

                    AINSWORTH
You mean just plain mental.

                    AINSWORTH
         (yelling)
That's a break everyone!

(muttering to himself)

Rotten no good lousy primadonna---

                              FOOTSTEPS APPROACHING

                    SWEETWATER
Let's ask this psychopath.

Sweetwater and Manetti approach Ainsworth.

                    SWEETWATER
Excuse me, I hate to interrupt your
breakdown---

                    AINSWORTH
         (annoyed)
How did you get on the set?

                    MANETTI
Well, I took-a da number 7 bus to West-
a 12th street. Den I transferred to da---

                    SWEETWATER
What Manetti means is, we're meeting
Miss Jamison. Allow me to introduce---

                    AINSWORTH
Don't care. Be gone! The director
never speaks to peasants, and peasants
are never allowed to speak the
director. There's a cameraman over
there, maybe he'll let you speak to
him.

                              FOOTSTEPS WALKING AWAY

                    MANETTI
He-a no very nice to you.

                    SWEETWATER
Well, you gotta understand that he's
probably high-strung, under a lot of
pressure, very creative and a total
jackass.

                    MANETTI
I can no unner-stand what he say. He
gotta dat accent. He no speak-a da
English good.

                    JAMISON
     (from a distance)
Oh gentlemen, you're here.

                    MANETTI
Why she tell-a us dat we here?

                    SWEETWATER
Maybe cause some of us aren't all
here.

                    JAMISON
     (agitated)
Have you seen the newspaper this
morning?

                    SWEETWATER
I'll have you know, I see the

newspaper every morning.

          MANETTI
Datsa right. He sees-a da paper every
day. He no read-a it. Joosta sees it.

          JAMISON
Then you didn't read what is on page
8? Here.

She hands a newspaper to Sweetwater.

                    SOUND OF NEWSPAPER RATTLING

          SWEETWATER
     (shocked)
Holy---.

          JAMISON
Exactly.

          MANETTI
What's-a goin' on boss?

          SWEETWATER
Carlson's hardware is having a great
sale on lawn mowers. I should get one.

          MANETTI
You no gotta lawn.

          SWEETWATER
True, but look at these prices. I'm
never gonna find one cheaper.

          JAMISON
     (pissed)
Not that. Above the ad.

          SWEETWATER
     (reading)
Movie star and Lover trash hotel
lobby... Aging movie actress, Heather
Jamison and her latest love interest,
local attorney, Sylvester Streetwater,
were seen sneaking into the Crown
Legacy Hotel late last night. When

spotted by the media the love birds
dashed through the throng, breaking
several priceless statues. Miss
Jamison is in town to film the movie
"Love Struck Out".

                    MANETTI
          Atsa not too bad.

                    JAMISON
               (still pissed)
          Are you kidding me? It's horrible.

                    SWEETWATER
          She's right, Manetti.

                    JAMISON
          Thank you.

                    SWEETWATER
          They got my name wrong.

                    JAMISON
               (livid)
          No, no, no! It's worse than that...

                    MANETTI
          Oh I know, dey call you and-a
          Streetwater, love-a birds?

                    JAMISON
          Hard to believe, but even worse than
          that.

                    SWEETWATER
          Very funny, Manetti. I think I'll sign
          your next check, Streetwater. Then
          we'll see how funny it is.

                    MANETTI
          Maybe da bank cash-a dat one. Dey no
          cash-a checks when you sign dem,
          Sweetwater.

                    JAMISON
          Can we get back to my problem?

                    MANETTI
          I thought Sweetwater was-a you
          problem?

                    JAMISON
They called me an aging actress!

                    SWEETWATER
How did the media know we were
sneaking in---

                    JAMISON
          (annoyed)
Did you hear what I said? They called
me an aging actress!

                    SWEETWATER
Don't worry my dear, you don't look
your age.

                    JAMISON
          (calmer)
Really?... How old do I look?

                    SWEETWATER
Fifty-three.

                    JAMISON
          (angrily)
I'm thirty-seven.

                    SWEETWATER
I said, you don't look your age...
Look I'd love to stay here and stroke
your ego, but I need to talk with your
entourage.

                    MANETTI
You mean we need-a to talk to dem.

                    SWEETWATER
You'll have to excuse Manetti. He has
this crazy idea that you are gonna
hire him instead of me.

                    JAMISON
Why can't I hire both of you?

                    MANETTI
Cause I can no work-a wid dis-a man.

                    JAMISON
Miss Rivers said you two always work
together.

               MANETTI
Oh, datsa right we do... I wonder who
it is I can-a no work-a wid.

               SWEETWATER
Maybe Jack the bookie.

               MANETTI
No, I work-a wid him fine. Maybe Big
Tony.

               JAMISON
Would you two please stop. Perhaps I
shouldn't hire either one of you since
you don't get along.

               MANETTI
We can work-a togeder.

               SWEETWATER
Yeah, we'll work together.

               JAMISON
Fine. I'll tell my entourage to be in
the hotel conference room in an hour.

               SWEETWATER
Great. Manetti, while I interview her
entourage... you interview... the rest
of the town.

                      TRANSITIONAL MUSIC

HOTEL CONFERENCE ROOM

                           DOOR OPENS

There are some conversations going on the conference room.

               SWEETWATER
This must be the conference room.

               MANETTI
               (from a distance)
Hey boss, wait-a for me.

                           RUNNING

               SWEETWATER
Manetti, you're supposed to be
interviewing the rest of the town.

                    MANETTI
          Oh, you said-a town? I tought you said-
          a interview da rest of da clowns. I no
          find any clowns.

                    SWEETWATER
          Let me get you a mirror... That must
          be the entourage over there.

CHARLIE OLIVER is talking with DARREN SIMS and PETE MCDOWELL.

                    SWEETWATER
          I'm Sylvester Sweetwater, are you the
          entourage for Heather Jamison?

                    CHARLIE
          Well, if you can call three people an
          entourage... I'm Charlie Oliver, Miss
          Jamison's personal assistant. This is
          Darren Sims, her publicist and Pete
          McDowell, her agent.

                    MANETTI
          Where are-a da other people?

                    DARREN
          There isn't anyone else. I'm sorry, I
          don't know who you are.

                    SWEETWATER
          Don't be sorry. I'm the one who should
          be sorry. I know who he is.

                    MANETTI
          My name is-a Giovanni Manetti, Private
          Detective---

                    SWEETWATER
          ---And public nuisance.

                    PETE
          Listen, none of us have any idea why
          Heather asked us to meet you. What is
          this all about?

                    SWEETWATER
          I'll ask the questions here.

                    MANETTI
Can-a I ask-a da question?

                    SWEETWATER
No. I said I'll ask the questions.

                    MANETTI
          (laughing)
Da joke-s she's-a on you. I joosta
asked da question!

                    SWEETWATER
Manetti, I think I hear your mom
calling you.

                    MANETTI
Really? You answer it den. She always
calls-a collect.

                    CHARLIE
Listen Mr. Sweetwater, we're all
really busy. So if you could get to
why we're here---

                    SWEETWATER
We were told there were more of you.

                    DARREN
There were, four years ago, when
Heather was one of the top grossing
actors in Hollywood.

                    CHARLIE
But since then...

                    PETE
Since then she hasn't really been
acting as much.

                    SWEETWATER
She believes that the one of you is
leaking things to the media.

                    CHARLIE
None of us would do something like
that. Well maybe, Darren.

                    DARREN
And that's my job as her publicist.
I'd love to have something to say to
the media about her. There's just no

interest.

                    SWEETWATER
What about that scene at the hotel
last night? They seemed to be
interested then.

                    DARREN
I have no idea what that was about. It
would have been great pub for her, if
you hadn't broken those statues.

                    MANETTI
Da boss, he no break-a dem. It was-a
some guy named Streetwater.

                    SWEETWATER
Miss Jamison thinks these leaks will
ruin her career.

                    PETE
I'm afraid that ship has sailed.

                    MANETTI
We no care about da ship. We care
about her career.

                    CHARLIE
With that said, we think that this
current project will jump start her
career.

                    DARREN
So really, if anything, these so-
called leaks are going to help.

                    PETE
Well, maybe. The screenplay still
sucks.

The Director, AINSWORTH enters.

                    AINSWORTH
Hey you three, where is your infernal
employer?

                    PETE
What?

                    MANETTI
          (to Pete)
I no unnerstand-a him either. He no
speak-a da good English like-a we do.

                    AINSWORTH
Heather Jamison. Where is she? I'm
ready to film her blasted scene, and
she's gone off to who knows where?

                    CHARLIE
          (panicked)
She's missing?

                    MANETTI
She's-a probably hidin' from-a da
media.

                    AINSWORTH
If she is missing, it will be bloody
great publicity for this God-awful
film.

                    SWEETWATER
Wait a minute... Do you happen to know
anything about all the leaks about her
in the media?

                    AINSWORTH
Know about 'em? Heck I planted the
ruddy things.

                              SOUNDS OF CONFUSED MUMBLING

                    SWEETWATER
You?

                    AINSWORTH
Of course. Listen mate, Heather
Jamison, my leading lady, hasn't been
relevant in four or five years. And
the other lead, Scott Tyler, he's flat
out nuts.

                    CHARLIE
That's an awful thing to do to Miss
Jamison! How could you be so cruel?

                        AINSWORTH
This film needs publicity before it
comes out, and it needs a big opening
weekend, cause once word gets out...
it's bombs away. Besides, Jamison
could use the exposure.

                        DARREN
We can never tell her. She'd be
crushed.

                        JAMISON
          (from a distance)
Tell me what? Be crushed about what?

                                        FOOT STEPS

                        DARREN
          (surprised)
Oh, Heather! I didn't see you standing
there.

                        JAMISON
Be crushed about what?

                        CHARLIE
Um---

                        PETE
Well---

                        MANETTI
Dey no wanna tell you dat da movie is-
a stinker.

                        JAMISON
          (laughing)
I already knew that... In fact all
these leaks about me will probably
help at the box office... until word
gets out, that is.

                        SWEETWATER
So the leaks don't bother you anymore?

                        JAMISON
No. In fact, it gave me a great
idea... My own reality show...
"Heather Jamison: Behind the Curtain".

                                TRANSITIONAL MUSIC

SWEETWATER AND KELP LAW OFFICES

TYPING

Miss Rivers is typing.

DOOR OPENS

FOOTSTEPS

Manetti enters the office.

            MANETTI
I gotta da mail for you, Miss-a
Rivers.

            RIVERS
Thank you, Mr. Manetti. I don't know
how I forgot it.

INTERCOM BUZZES

            SWEETWATER
             (through intercom)
Miss Rivers, did you get the mail this
morning?

            MANETTI
It's-a right here, boss.

DOOR OPENS

FOOTSTEPS

Sweetwater joins them.

            SWEETWATER
Oh Manetti, you're here.
             (To Rivers)
I thought I told you to get the locks
changed.

            MANETTI
Looks-a like you gotta something from
Miss Jamison.

                    SWEETWATER
Gimme that.

                    SOUND OF SORTING AND FALLING ENVELOPES

                    SWEETWATER
Ah, here it is.

                    MANETTI
She no forget-a you.

                    RIVERS
I wonder what it is?

                    SWEETWATER
Probably a marriage proposal. Poor
confused kid.

                              ENVELOPE OPENING

                    MANETTI
What is-a it, boss?

                    SWEETWATER
          (somewhat dejected)
An autographed picture and three
tickets to the premiere of "Love
Struck Out".

                    RIVERS
That's sweet!

                    MANETTI
She's-a right. When is-a da premiere?

                    SWEETWATER
Friday at 7:00 at the Cedar Theater.

                    MANETTI
We gonna go, right?

                    SWEETWATER
I dunno, Friday at 7? They'll be big
crowds. I'd rather wait until the hype
dies down a bit.

                    MANETTI
Okay, how about the 9:00 show on
Friday?

                    SWEETWATER
          Perfect.

-The End-

END CREDITS

                                        FADE IN END CREDITS

                    THE VOICE OF THE CLEVELAND RADIO PLAYERS
          This is Denny Castiglione ladies and
          gentlemen, You've been listening to
          The Cleveland Radio Players
          Performance of The Sweetwater Files,
          Private Instigator Starring...

                    JACK MATUSZEWSKI
          (as Sylvester Sweetwater)

                    DINA KARALNIK
          (as Miss Rivers)

                    MILTON HOROWITZ
          (As Giovanni Manetti)

                    ERIC SEVER
          (as Malcolm Ainsworth)

                    SONIA RESTIVO
          (As Miss Jamison)

                    GIOVANNI CASTIGLIONE
          (As Charlie)

                    BARNABAS BRENNAN
          (As Pete)

                    DAVID FLYNT
          (As Darren)

          This Episode was Written and Directed
          by Jimmy Pelyhes Recorded live at BAD
          RACKET STUDIOS copyright 20017.

THE END
          To listen to Sweetwater Files 3:
          Private Investigator as a radio play,
          please visit
          www.clevelandradioplayers.com

Rights and Royalties

Originally adapted for the radio and performed by The Cleveland Radio Players.

Written and directed by Jim Pelyhes

Recorded at Bad Racket Studios

For more information on performance rights and royalties, or to listen to *Sweetwater Files: Private Investigator* as a radio play, please visit www.ClevelandRadioPlayers.com

www.ingramcontent.com/pod-product-compliance
Lightning Source LLC
Chambersburg PA
CBHW080812120626
46556CB00009B/3301